Secret
Places

BRITTANY MAE

ISBN:0692916296
ISBN-13:9780692916292

CONTENTS

CHAPTER ONE

My favorite song comes on half-way through my walk to Mom's cafe. Ahhh, Rachmaninoff, his piano playing is a gift from the gods. I close my eyes for a moment as his music transports me to the clouds, and I let the Saturday afternoon sun radiate on my skin. I'm weightless for a minute, but a poke on my right shoulder forces me back to the concrete of the highway road.

"Hey." The boy speaks, and I turn around to face him. We lock eyes for only a second, as I immediately look down. He's handsome. I feel my face get hot as I assume embarrassment will be in my near future. Talking to people is my worst nightmare.

"I'm James."

"Hi."

My voice cracks. I keep staring at my feet. I take out my left earphone to be polite, but keep the other one in to show that I'm not willing to talk for more than a minute. Also, Rachmaninoff in my right ear is calming me.

"I was… I was actually just wondering how to get to Main Street Cafe?"

My insides start shaking. This answer requires more than three words. I take a deep breath, but never exhale. "You walk straight up this road for about ten minutes, and then you'll see Main Street and the cafe on the left." My thudding heart made my voice shake. That's Mom's cafe, and I know my answer is right, but I had to say more than three words.

"Oh, thank you."

I nod politely and replace the other earphone in my ear as I continue walking up the highway. Tears start welling up in my eyes as a repercussion of having to speak, but I've become a pro at sucking them back in. I count, one, two, three, four, five. My eyes are already dry. It used to take me until I reached ten to get the tears to stop. As I continue walking, I analyze the entire conversation, mentally punching myself for blushing, shaking, and then tearing up again. I could have at least made eye contact. He could've become my friend. Mom has been nagging me to at least make one friend, but I think Mom's the only friend I really need. She's the only one I can actually trust.

Then, I surprise myself. I turn around to face James, who is several feet behind me. I don't know what came over me, maybe it was Mom's nagging in my head, or the overwhelmingly powerful aura of Rachmaninoff, or a combination of both, but some unconscious force caused me to start walking back to him. When I approached him, we locked eyes again, but I couldn't keep contact for more than three seconds before looking down again. Well, at least that's two seconds longer than earlier.

"I'm actually going to the cafe, so you can follow me if you want." Did I just invite him to walk next to me? Now I'm going to have to participate in small talk. I didn't think this through.

"Really? Yeah, that would be great, thank you."

James walks to the left of me as I lead the way up the road. A few silent minutes pass, and I'm grateful he hasn't spoken. I sense him jerking every time a car whizzes past us at forty miles per hour, so I hand him my left earphone without saying a word and without making eye contact. He puts it in his right ear, and we continue up the highway, drowning out car engines with the delicate ambiance of piano keys. As we approach the door to Mom's cafe, a generic ringtone sounds off in James's back pocket.

"It's my Mom."

While he answers the text, I wait and mostly look at the ground, occasionally sneaking a glance at his face. He has electric blue eyes.

"Uhhh, I have to go actually. My mom wants me to come back and get a head start on my homework before dinner."

"You have school in the middle of August?" The idea of starting my senior year early in the hell hole they call high school makes my insides jitter in disgust.

"Yeah, I just started last week. My mom says if I start earlier I can end earlier."

"Where do you go to school?" I never ask questions. Questions are an invitation for more conversation. I was curious though. I've lived in Greenwood since I was born, and I thought the only high school that was here was the dreaded one I go to.

"Well... I'm homeschooled actually... and my mom teaches me... so..."

"Oh."

"Yeah. Well, I'm gonna have to start walking back... Thank you for..."

"Wait, you should at least try one of the cookies in there. They're pretty amazing." As I say that, I start walking quickly into Mom's cafe. I walk around the counter and grab a chocolate chip cookie from behind the display case. James is still waiting as I rush out of the cafe.

"Here." Still afraid to make eye contact, I look down at his hands as I give it to him.

"Thank you! Uh, did you pay for this?"

"Don't worry, I know the woman who owns it."

"Oh, okay cool. Well, thank you so much for the help earlier. Maybe I'll see you around?"

"Yeah, I walk here every Saturday… so." Did I just invite him to walk with me again? I'm really shocking myself today.

"I'll keep that in mind. Oh, what is your name by the way?"

"Rosalie." Could he actually be interested in my invitation?

"Rosalie. Cool. See ya around!"

He turns around to walk back down the road, and I walk back into Mom's cafe.

"Who was that cookie for?" Mom can't hide her smirk as she pulls me behind the

counter. She's been begging me to make a friend for years.

"Oh. Just some guy."

"A guy?! I didn't see him! Is he cute?" I notice Mom's brown eyes widen as her smile stretches to her ears.

"Mom. Relax. Stop getting your hopes up."

Still grinning, Mom sighs sarcastically. I know she never stops hoping, and I hate disappointing her.

CHAPTER TWO

James stretches his fingers out towards me, and my fingers unconsciously respond to his magnetic force, intertwining mine with his. We are midway through my extensive backyard, nearing the division strip at the end where the row of tall trees begins. I walk a little slower than normal, as I'm hesitant to reach this division line, and I think James notices. He doesn't mention it though, and his patience assures me about crossing that division line. This is the first time I'm bringing someone to my spot. It's only been a little over a month since I've met him, but I have convinced myself that he's worthy of accompanying me. We reach the division, and I make the first step over the line into the extended abyss of the woods. James eagerly follows my movements.

We both remain silent as we walk, and I listen to the leaves and sticks crunch below us with each step we take. It's September 30th, and leaves have already begun to fall. I remember the first time I walked along this path. It was almost five years ago, the day I decided to completely disregard Dad for the rest of time. We wander down my usual, straight path, and I make an effort to step in the patches of sunlight peeking through gaps in the trees. Those patches provide some appreciated warmth, as well as some light for guidance through the mostly darkened area. James remains diagonally behind me, letting me have all of the sunlight.

My pace quickens as I continue forward, grateful for James's deftness as he follows me. It's convincing me that it's okay for him to be here. I've been trying desperately to open myself up to him, but the only other man I've ever trusted, or even had close contact with, was Dad, but he had proven himself unworthy countless times.

An involuntary image of wasted Dad blinds me from the present. He's driving up to the parking lot of my middle school and struggling out of the driver's seat. I was only twelve at the time, but I could tell he was having trouble standing, and saw him desperately gripping the sides of the car for support as he started to walk around it and towards me. He was good at hiding his drunkenness by that point in his life. I could tell he was drunk, but anyone that doesn't know how he acted sober would've just thought he's a little strange. He caught my gaze.

"Marie!" he exclaimed. Marie is Mom's name. I immediately shifted my eyes in any other other direction but his, and stood there, completely frozen.

"Hey you! Don't ignore me. I'm gonna drive you to our house." I recall a slight slur in his voice, and I was just standing there, eyes downward, planning out how to escape.

"Rosalie!"

He said my name. Everyone's eyes fixated on me, and their gazes felt like the atmosphere was pressing on my skull and squeezing my lungs. I involuntarily walked to the car. The overwhelming pressure from innumerable stares, combined with fact that he actually said my name for the first time in a while, forced me forward. When I reached him, he put his hand on my shoulder and used it for support as he opened the door to the passenger side, still leaning on me as I got in. He slowly drove out of my school's parking lot and into a two way intersection, where he turned right.

"Our house is the other way, Dad." I said quietly.

"Oh don't worry honey, I'm taking the shortcut way.

I knew there was no "shortcut way" in the direction we were going, but I just sat there quietly. He was driving very slowly, with a few sharp breaks here and there. The car was slightly swerving side to side, but, impressively, he was able to keep it within our lane. With every break and swerve, my heart dropped to my stomach, and then back up again. That feeling reenters my present self, straining my chest and forcing me back to reality.

I'm still leading James down the right path. My inner compass must have put my unconscious mind into autopilot. I consider the thought of James following me from behind, sending my heart into a beating uproar of nerves and self-consciousness, but I try to brush it away by focusing on the sounds of leaves crunching and soft squeals from the slight breeze that passes my ears.

"You look beautiful, Rosalie."

James ends the silence. His words break my concentration, and I turn around to face him, unable to release my magnetized fingers from his. My eyes lock onto his, and he hypnotizes me into stillness and silence for a brief moment. I feel my face warm and the bottoms of my eyelids fill with water, but I count to five and blink it away. I inhale without ever exhaling, and my heart drops to my stomach. I have to say something, but the only words I could force out of my mouth were, "Thank you". My voice cracks as I say it. Did he even hear what I said? James blushes, I probably terrified him, but he genuinely smiles and nods his head. Overwhelmed with embarrassment, I immediately turn around and continue forward, fixing my gaze straight ahead, with James walking close behind me. The last time a man said I was beautiful was that time wasted Dad drove me home from middle school.

He was driving down an unfamiliar road when he slurred the words, "You look beautiful today, dear."

"You missed a stop sign." My twelve year old self tried to sound as uninterested as I could.

"You are really growing up aren't you, Rosalie?" He said my name. "Your hair is so beautiful. It's a wonderful shade of brown. I love it long and down like that."

I remember I paused before I answered, shocked at the fact that he said my name. He actually acknowledged my existence.

"Thank you." I involuntarily smiled as I said that.

"Do you have a boyfriend?"

"No."

"Well, if you turn eighteen and don't

have a boyfriend, can I take you out? I'll take you to some bars." He was beaming when he said that.

"I can't drink until I'm twenty-one," I was confused at the time.

"That's okay, we'll dress you up. You're going to look beautiful. They will definitely let you in." He placed his hand on my bare leg. The car swerved to the right.

"Okay..." I remember being pretty confused still, considering I was only twelve. I turned my knees toward the passenger door and his fell away.

"I'm looking forward to showing you off! My beautiful Rosalie!" He said my name again.

A loud crunch from a stick below me takes me back to my walk with James. We are still on the right path, and I realize that we are nearing my spot. I involuntarily slow down, still hesitant about actually following through with this. James gently rubs his thumb along my hand, and it sends my heart into a jittery flutter, reminding me of a different kind of flutter my heart endured when wasted Dad was steering a quickly accelerating car.

He was speeding down a narrow curvy road, aligned with trees on either side, and I remember the car tipping as he rounded the sharp curves. I was sitting there, frozen, with my heart dropping to my feet. I became numb, unsure of what to say or do to get the car into control. I shutter at Dad's obnoxious laugh in my head. He was acting like he was on a roller coaster. I remember seeing another car a far distance ahead coming towards us and honking incessantly. They were going to hit us in seconds. In that moment, my adrenaline kicked in, and I instinctively grabbed the wheel and turned it sharply to the left. A few seconds later, Dad hit the brakes.

The sharp jolt of the braking car

caused my present self to jump, and I blink the images out of my mind to notice the narrow stream with the curved tree branch hanging over it, and my favorite sitting rock on the side nearest me. I lead James to the rock and, still holding his hand, drag him down to sit next to me. We lean our backs against the giant boulder, with our legs stretched out in front of us. I hear James breathing deeply. I must have quickened my pace.

Self-conscious thoughts crowd my brain again. What has James been thinking this entire walk? Was he bored? Does he think this is ridiculous? Did he stare at me the entire time? The thought of him staring at me from behind is the most frightening thought. What if he notices my flaws? I count to five and brush those anxieties away, closing my eyes and hoping to blend into the environment. Maybe I could even melt into the ground. Counting to five wasn't enough this time, as I grow more anxious with images that blur my vision to reveal where the car ended up after Dad hit the brakes.

The car stopped very suddenly onto the edge of where a forest began. We had missed the other car by mere inches, and the other car had continued forward, still honking, with the driver yelling incoherent words out his window.

I remember Dad was still laughing in that obnoxious tone before he let out a sigh, "That was a close one! I knew I could count on you, my dear Marie!"

That was it for me. That was the moment I realized I no longer had a father. It was the moment I realized that I needed to not only ignore him, but to avoid him as if he was a demon. My body was numb at that point, and I couldn't see or hear, but I vaguely remember getting out of the car and running into the woods. Dad was yelling slurred and unclear words in the distance, but he didn't bother to run after me. I left him there, and didn't care if he ever made it back home. While running through the woods, I ended up at what has become my favorite spot. I remember that moment clearly, and that familiar feeling of leaning against the boulder and melting into the earth. It was able to calm my hysterical sobs as I tried to recover from the worst hour I had ever experienced.

James erases my turbulent mind as he reaches his arm around my shoulder, pulling me in close. Instead of melting into the earth, I feel myself melting into him, and I release my weight into his side and rest my head into the dip where his neck meets his shoulder. He rests his chin on my head. His embrace seems to be the only thing today that can cease my consistent inner turmoil. I exhale and close my eyes, listening to the water crashing over the rocks and back into the stream. My mind finally calms into a blank state, and I'm able to reach a rare serene stillness.

"I'm glad you're here." I whisper

quietly. The words unconsciously poured out of me, and I count to ten to calm my racing heart. It's been one month of us hanging out, and I've never admitted out loud any sort of likeness or appreciation towards him.

"I really like you a lot," He responds, and his voice is a little shaky, "and since it's been a month…"

I know what He's going to say, this question is inevitable. At least he's waited a while to ask, but I'm still unsure of how to answer. Not wanting to look at him, I remain very still with my eyes closed, noticing the vibrations of his shaking voice on my head.

"…is it okay to ask you to be my girlfriend?"

There it was. The words I've been dreading. Of course I want to tell him yes, but I'm afraid of what comes after that. Mom loved Dad, and it destroyed her. Mom had often confided in me with matters concerning Dad's alcoholic issues. Within these conversations, I always learned some sort of lesson about relationships, which I have always remembered. It's the reason I've vowed to myself to stay away from men. Mom tried to be honest with Dad, telling him he's stopped helping around the house, that he needs to work at the cafe, and that he drinks too much, but she always paid the price. He would laugh at her, say she's lying, and tell her she's a paranoid schizophrenic. What's even worse is that Mom actually started to believe she was crazy, and would constantly ask me for reassurance, to which I would obviously tell her she's perfect. She's a compassionate, generous, and dangerously forgiving woman, but she loved Dad unconditionally, and always had a false hope that he would change. I desperately held on to this false hope as well, of course until that day he tried to drunkenly drive me home. Before then, I had been blinded to the fact that I was nonexistent in his eyes. He rarely looked at me, and if he did acknowledge me, he was mistaking me for Mom in his drunken delirious state, and yelling about things that I usually did not understand. He's the only man I've ever had a sort of relationship with, and my parents' relationship is the only real one I've ever seen, other than the fantasy kinds on TV. If only those were true.

I really like James though. After all, I've brought him to my spot. Every time I touch him, or am even near him for that matter, I feel an undeniable magnetic force radiating between us. With every day I've been with him, my need to have him keeps growing stronger, and it scares me. He's the only friend I've had in years, and spending time with him has been refreshing. School has been less dreadful with him to look forward to at the end of each day. Evenings alone in my house while Mom works at the cafe have been less lonely with him by my side. He respects my need to remain mostly quiet and willingly sits with me in silence when we take walks, watch TV, or work on homework. Despite this silence, he's actually gotten me to talk more as weeks have passed. Usually if I speak to anyone but Mom, my voice cracks, my cheeks turn red, and my eyes fill with tears. After a few weeks of talking to James, I've been able to talk to him and everyone else with a little more confidence and a little less blushing and tearing. He's also gotten me to laugh, like really laugh. Not my usual half-hearted laugh, where I force a half-smile and let out some humming sounds, but the kind only Mom can get me to do, where giggles uncontrollably pour out of my wide open mouth in a discordant symphony. There's also his eyes. My pupils lock onto his blue irises like magnets, and it's hard to disconnect from his gaze. He's always so honest and straightforward, and I can see those qualities exuding through his eyes. There's also no greater feeling than leaning into his side as he wraps his arm around me in a warm, snug embrace. It's like a forcefield for my anxiety, blocking my inner chaos and allowing my mind to rest. I'm safe. In a world where love can lie as a hobby, destroy sanity, and drink until it dies, I just want to feel safe. He provides that.

"It's gonna get dark soon, we should start going." I can't say yes. Anxiety has strangled me.

"It's only four. We have another hour at least." I notice his voice is quieter now, but still a little shaky. I feel terrible; I can tell in his voice that he's discouraged.

"Yeah, but it's getting cold. I'm really cold." It's the first excuse that popped into my head. I start to stand up. It's the first time I've moved since leaning into him.

"Oh. Well, okay. We should leave then." James starts standing up too.

I glance at him quickly, and notice the despair on his face, but I begin walking, and he follows closely behind. Every step I take gets heavier, and I contemplate the risks of just saying the word 'yes'. Anxieties overwhelm my brain once again, so I starting counting. One, two, three, four, five, six, seven, eight, nine, ten… the thoughts aren't ceasing. With a desperate need to calm myself, I extend my arm behind me, fingers stretched out towards James. That force pulls our palms together, sticking us like glue.

"Yes." I stop sharply in my tracks. The word had forced itself out of me before I could finish thinking. I turn around to face him.

"Oh… Are you sure?" James is beaming, but his lips are quivering. I could tell he was trying to downplay his excitement.

"Yes, I'm sure." With that, I immediately turn around. I feel my face get warm again, but this time my eyes are dry, and my mouth unconsciously stretches from ear to ear.

CHAPTER THREE

As I continue through the seasons with James, the world around me grows brighter and more colorful than I thought was possible. With each passing day, my inner turmoil lessens, and I begin to feel as if I'm floating, but James is the weight that keeps me from escaping into the sky. We spend every afternoon and evening together, and when the weather is nice enough, we relax in my favorite spot for hours. Before him, I was machine, going through ordinary daily routines, struggling to forget the past, but fearing the future. With him, the past disappears from my mind, allowing me to look forward to a promising future filled with love and security. I used to be afraid of everyone and everything around me, but he has proven that trust is not something to be feared. His voice illuminates my soul, and his kisses breathe new life into me. I need him.

With our fingers intertwined, James and I reach our favorite spot. Leaves crunch below us as I lead him towards our sitting rock. We have made it to another September. I encourage him to lean against the rock as I sit across from him. James locks his eyes onto me, and I am hypnotized by his electric blue irises. He's unreal. We gaze at each other for a brief moment, and then I place the small box I was carrying in both hands on the ground in front of him. It's wrapped in silver wrapping paper.

"Okay," I exhale, "I know my tendency towards silence probably left you feeling confused and worried most of the time, but I hope this makes up for it."

James sighs and laughs, nodding his head in agreement that he was most certainly confused for a while. He takes the box and carefully begins pulling the tape off of the silver wrapping. I can't handle the suspense, and I giggle, "Just rip it!" James begins ripping the paper open, revealing an envelope-sized white box. He opens the box to see a note placed on top of a silver envelope.

My Dearest James,

I often didn't give you the reassurance you needed, but you never stopped reassuring me of your loyalty and honesty. Even though I didn't say these feelings out loud, I always wrote them down in a notebook. The envelope contains pages from this notebook, and I hope they give you the reassurance you deserve. I fell in love with you so quickly, and I think these pages will prove it to you. Thank you for being patient, for sticking by me, and for making me feel safe. Happy one year! I love you.

Love,

Rosalie

James is beaming. His immediate expression looks as if he won the lottery, but it quickly switches to one of concern.

"This is more than I need, Rosalie. Are you sure?"

"You deserve this. I trust you."

He smiles and carefully places the note back on top of the envelope and closes the box, gently placing it in his lap.

"I'll read these later. It's my turn."

James hands me a light blue drawstring bag. It's heavy. I tug the strings to open it and pull out a small rock with words painted on it in white.

"Your hypnotizing brown eyes". I unconsciously smile as I read it.

"I've been collecting a small rock from this spot every time we come here. I know that's a lot of rocks, so I narrowed it down to twenty. They all have reasons why I love you painted on them."

My eyes fill with water as I allow my mouth to stretch into the largest smile I've ever formed. For the first time in my life, instead of tearing from anxiety and fear, I am tearing out of pure joy.

"This is better than I could've imagined." I really meant that.

I reach over and start kissing James's face from his cheeks, to his lips, to his neck. James is laughing. "Woah, woah, woah there! Don't thank me yet." He pulls a tiny drawstring bag out of his front jean pocket and places it in my palm. I'm confused, but incredibly excited. I stretch open the bag and pull out a small, golden ring with a round sapphire jewel in the center. My eyes widen as I gaze at the shiny stone in wonderment. I tilt the ring side to side in my fingers, making it glisten in different places as it catches the light.

"It's a promise." James begins to explain. "If you ever need reassurance, I want you to look at it and remember my true love and dedication for you. I promise to remain truthful and loyal, and my love for you will never falter."

"Are you sure about this?" I've now convinced myself that I'm probably dreaming. A year ago I would've laughed at the thought of actually being in a relationship, especially with a guy like this. It just seemed too impossible.

"I've been sure for over a year."

I smile and lift my eyes to lock them into his. James reaches over to hold my head in his hands and kisses my lips gently. I turn myself around and lean against his chest, sliding the ring onto my ring finger. James rests his chin on my head and wraps his arms around me. I'm safe.

CHAPTER FOUR

A few days pass into Tuesday evening, and James and I are cooking Alfredo pasta in my kitchen. I hear the front door open, and assume it's my mom coming back from work early. That's very unusual.

"Mom?"

"Yes, sweetie. It's me. The cafe wasn't too crowded tonight, so I left a little early. Amy and George seemed to have a good handle on the few customers that are there."

Mom walks into the kitchen and kisses

me on the forehead.

"Whatcha making?"

"Alfredo pasta. James is making the chicken."

"James?" I notice her brown eyes widen as she smiles with excited surprise. She's never met James. I've been too afraid to tell her about him, but I feel secure in telling her now. He's promised to stay with me for a while.

"Yeah, we've been hanging out for a while."

"Oh! Where is he? I want to meet him!"

I laugh, "Uh, he's right there at the stove, Mom."

James turns around and walks towards Mom. He's smiling politely, but I can feel that he's nervous.

"Hi! It's nice to finally meet you. I've

been really looking forward to this opportunity." He reaches out his hand, but Mom doesn't respond to his gesture. She keeps staring at the stove with her eyebrows frowning in a confused expression.

James quickly drops his hand and rushes towards the stove, "Oh, the stove! I'm so sorry, I promise it's not burning."

"Mom!" I look at her confused, and a little angry, "You could have at least shaken his hand." Mom is always so sweet and outgoing. How could she not like him? She likes everyone!

Mom blinks away from the stove and looks over at me, "Sorry. I must be really exhausted. I think I'm going to take a nap upstairs."

"Yeah, you seem tired. I'll save you some pasta." She must be really out of it.

"Thank you, sweetie."

Mom leaves and goes upstairs.

"Did I screw up? You always say how talkative she is. I shouldn't have walked away with the stove burner on." James looks at me, and the despair on his face is a little endearing. He really wants her to like him.

"No, you were perfect. She's just exhausted. Don't worry about it, she wasn't herself." I kiss him on the cheek, and he smiles slightly with relief. I'm actually grateful she isn't eating with us, I prefer to spend time alone with James anyways.

CHAPTER FIVE

"Please just let me wait for him to come here!" I'm hysterically crying as my distressed mother carries my suitcase to the front door.

"He's not coming, Rosalie. You have to believe me."

My chest heaves with my hysteria, and I answer her in short spurts. "NO! You have to… believe… ME. He… comes here at… 12 on Saturdays. It's… 11:45. Please… just give me fifteen minutes."

"How about we stop by his house on the way?"

"I don't know where he lives, I told you that!"

"Exactly, and why is that?"

"He always says my house is better. We always hang out here!"

"No, sweetheart. We have gone over this. James doesn't exist."

"MOMMM! He does! You have to believe me!"

I follow Mom outside and stand several feet behind her as she loads the suitcase into the trunk. Mom opens the passenger car door for me, but I refuse to move. She grabs my arm and tries to gently drag me into the seat, then walks around to the driver's side and gets in. She starts the car.

"I'm sorry sweetheart, but I can't. Dr.

Johnson said you're going to have to trust me. Once we get you settled in, she's going to help you. She's a really kind woman and a great listener…"

"Dr. Johnson doesn't know! S he's never met James! But YOU have met him!"

"Rosalie, I didn't meet him."

"Yes, you did! I introduced him to you last week. He was cooking dinner with me. He was so sweet to you, and you ignored him!"

"I know you don't believe me, but I didn't see him."

"Mom, I swear. Are you blind? He even talked to you! Maybe YOU'RE the one that's crazy!"

"I told you, I thought I was going crazy. I truly did. Then you kept having him over to cook dinner with you a few more times, and every time I came home to you telling me that James was there, I still never saw him or heard him. So I called our doctor, Dr. Bates, who referred me to Dr. Johnson and Dr. Johnson said…"

"STOP! You already told me this. She said I was crazy! I'm NOT crazy!"

"She never said you were crazy, sweetheart. She said you could have developed this mentality as a form of coping with…"

"I KNOW, Mom! It's all Dad's fault! He made me like this! That's what she said, right?! Well, that's a lie. How could someone that didn't pay any attention to me, affect me? That man has been dead to me before he was even dead."

With that, Mom fell into complete silence. I notice her knuckles turn whiter as she clenches the steering wheel a little harder. Uncontrollable sobs continue to pour out of me, as I mentally list the reasons why James is real. I could see him. I could hear him. I could feel him. That feeling of our fingers intertwined, with warm palms pressed together is real. Those electric blue irises that hypnotize me, making me feel as though I caught a glimpse of his soul. Definitely real. His warm embrace. My ability to melt into him. Certainly not fake. He makes me feel safe. Without him, I'm not safe.

I refocus my teary eyes as I gaze out the window. A sign on the right reads, "Johnson Psychiatric Institution". Mom turns right and pulls into the parking lot. I see James standing at the edge of where the lot meets the front pathway leading to the entrance. As soon as Mom stops the car, I push open the door and sprint to James. My hysterical sobs grow louder as I wrap my arms around James.

"I'm so glad you found me!"

James remains silent and squeezes me as I rest my head on his chest and close my eyes. I hear Mom rolling my suitcase from behind, and a woman's gentle voice in front of me.

"Hi there, are you Rosalie?"

I remain silent, never releasing my grasp from James.

"Yes, this is Rosalie," Mom says from behind me. Her voice is shaking. "Are you Dr. Johnson?"

"Yes, that's me. Well, we are happy to have you stay here, Rosalie. I understand you're nervous, but I promise we will help you feel comfortable."

Dr. Johnson gently touches my right shoulder, and I remain frozen with my eyes smashed shut, never letting go of James.

Mom whispers from behind me, "It's safe in there, sweetheart, I promise."

I open my eyes to see Dr. Johnson smiling at me calmly. James is no longer in front of me. I take her hand.

ABOUT THE AUTHOR

Brittany Mae is an emerging young author. Growing up in the Hudson Valley as a dancer, artist and writer, her childhood hometown is often the backdrop of her work. She currently resides in Brooklyn, New York